A Hippo
in Our Yard

A Hippo in Our Yard

Liza Donnelly

Holiday House / New York

Mom, we have a hippo
in our yard.

I don't think so, dear.

I will give it
some lettuce.

Here you go, Miss Hippo.

Maybe later.

I will give it some tuna.

Here you go, Mr. Tiger.

Liz, we have
zebras
in our garage!
We do!
Come see!

Not now. Go away.
I am texting Patty.

I will give them some carrots.

Here you go, zebra family!

Nana, we have koalas in our hammock!

That's nice, dear.

Want to see?

No, I believe you.
It sounds fun.
You can give them
some grapes.

Everyone
stay inside!
The zoo animals
got out!

Where is Sally?

For Ella and Gretchen

Library of Congress Cataloging-in-Publication Data

Donnelly, Liza, author, illustrator.
A hippo in our yard / Liza Donnelly. — First edition.
        pages cm.
Summary: "Sally tries to tell her family that a hippo, a tiger, zebras
and koalas are in their yard, but no one pays attention until they
hear that the zoo animals have escaped; now everyone panics
except for Sally!"— Provided by publisher.
ISBN 978-0-8234-3564-7 (hardcover)
[1. Zoo animals—Fiction.] I. Title.
PZ7.D7195Hi 2016
[E]—dc23

2015022328